Millie
Waits
for the
Mail

First published as *Lieselotte Lauert* in 2006 by Patmos Verlag, Germany.

No part of this publication may be reproduced, stored in a retrieval system, or transmitted in any form or by any means, electronic, mechanical, photocopying, recording, or otherwise, without written permission of the publisher. For information regarding permission, write to Walker Publishing Company, Inc., 175 Fifth Avenue, New York, NY 10010.

ISBN-13: 978-0-545-15211-2
ISBN-10: 0-545-15211-9

Text and illustrations: Alexander Steffensmeier. Copyright © 2006 by Patmos Verlag GmbH & Co. KG. Sauerländer Verlag, Düsseldorf. Translation copyright © 2007 by Patmos Verlag. All rights reserved. Published by Scholastic Inc., 557 Broadway, New York, NY 10012, by arrangement with Walker Publishing Company, Inc. SCHOLASTIC and associated logos are trademarks and/or registered trademarks of Scholastic Inc.

12 11 10 9 8 7 6 5 4 3 2   9 10 11 12 13 14/0

Printed in the U.S.A.   40

First Scholastic printing, February 2009

Millie
Waits for the
Mail

Alexander
Steffensmeier

SCHOLASTIC INC.
New York Toronto London Auckland Sydney
Mexico City New Delhi Hong Kong Buenos Aires

Every morning while being milked,
Millie stared out at the farmyard.

This was her favorite
time of day. Because there was
something Millie loved more
than anything else—

scaring the mail carrier . . . .

. . . and chasing him off the farm.

Every day
Millie searched
for a new hiding place.

On the days the farmer didn't get any mail,
Millie felt so let down.

The farmer
didn't share
Millie's idea of fun.

All her
packages

arrived broken.

Millie had to be stopped.

And the mail carrier had terrible nightmares every night.

But one morning, he finally had
an idea.

"Maybe if I bring
the cow a package,"
he said to himself,
"she will like me."

The next day, Millie lay in wait,
just as she did every morning.

And Millie scared the mail carrier, just as she did
every morning.

"That's

enough!" shouted the farmer,

chasing after Millie,
who was chasing after
the mail carrier . . . again.

"Stop right there!"

"Enough already!"
shouted the mail carrier too.
"This package is for *you,*
you silly cow."

Millie slid to a sudden stop.
A package? She had never
received a package before.
What on earth
could it be?

The box bounced right past her
and landed under the wheels of the
farmer's tractor.

"Oh, no!" yelled the
farmer, but it was too
late.

The package was completely flattened.

Millie's heart dropped and her feet went out from under her.

And when she pulled herself up on wobbly knees, the mail carrier's bicycle looked a little different.

"I'm ruined," sniffed the mail carrier. "How will I deliver the mail without my bicycle?"

Now, every morning Millie can't wait to finish her milking. Because there is something she loves more than anything else—

delivering the mail.